I Can Read with My Eyes Shut!

I Can Read with My Eyes Shut!

By

Dr. Seuss

RANDOM HOUSE 🏠 NEW YORK

Published in the United States by Random House Children's Books,
a division of Random House, Inc., New York.

Random House and colophon are registered trademarks of Random House, Inc.

www.randomhouse.com/kids
www.seussville.com
www.kohlscorporation.com

Educators and librarians, for a variety of teaching tools, visit us at
www.randomhouse.com/teachers

This special edition was printed for Kohl's by Random House Children's Books,
a division of Random House, Inc., New York.

ISBN: 978-0-375-85380-7

MANUFACTURED IN CHINA
10 9 8 7 6 5 4 3 2 1

For

David Worthen, E.G.*

*(Eye Guy)

I can read
in red.

I can read
in blue.

I can read in
pickle color
too.

I can read in bed.

And in purple.
And in brown.

I can read
with
my
left eye.

I
can
read
with
my right.

I can read
Mississippi
with my eyes shut tight!

Mississippi

Mississippi,

Indianapolis

and

Hallelujah,

too!

I can read them
with my eyes shut!

That is
VERY HARD
to do!

But it's bad for my hat
and makes my eyebrows
get red hot.

SO . . .

reading with my eyes shut
I don't do an awful lot.

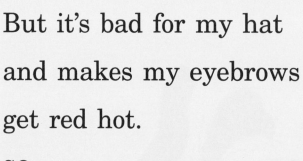

And when I keep them open
I can read with much more speed.
You have to be a speedy reader
'cause there's so, so much to read!

You can read about trees . . .

and bees . . .

and knees.

And knees on trees!

And
bees
on
threes!

You can read about anchors.

And all about ants.

You can read
about ankles!

And crocodile pants!

You can read about hoses . . .

and how

to smell roses . . .

and what
you should do
about owls on noses!

Young cat! If you keep
your eyes open enough,
oh, the stuff you will learn!
The most wonderful stuff!

You'll learn about . . .

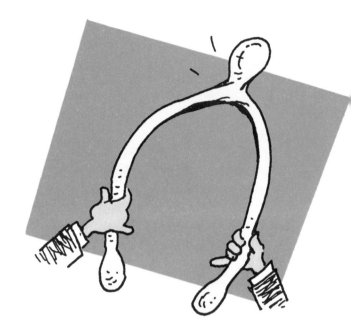

fishbones . . .   and wishbones.

You'll learn
about trombones,
too.

You'll learn
about Jake
the Pillow Snake

and all about
Foo-Foo the Snoo.

You can learn about ice.

You can learn about mice.

Mice on ice.

And
ice
on
mice.

You can learn about
the price of ice.

Nice ice
for sale.
Ten cents a pail.

You can learn about SAD . . .

and GLAD . . .

and MAD!

There are
so many things
you can learn about.
BUT . . . you'll miss
the best things
if you keep
your eyes shut.

The more that you read,

the more things you will know.

The more that you learn,

the more places you'll go.

You might learn
a way to earn
a few dollars.

Or how to make doughnuts . . .

or kangaroo collars.

You can learn to read music
and play a Hut-Zut
if you keep your eyes open.
But <u>not</u> with them shut.

If you read with your eyes shut
you're likely to find
that the place where you're going
is far, far behind.

SO . . .

that's why I tell you

to keep your eyes wide.

Keep them wide open . . .

at least on one side.